The Dolphin Caller

Story by Don Campbell
Illustrations by Meredith Thomas

Contents

Prologue	4
Chapter One	5
Chapter Two	10
Chapter Three	22
Epilogue	30

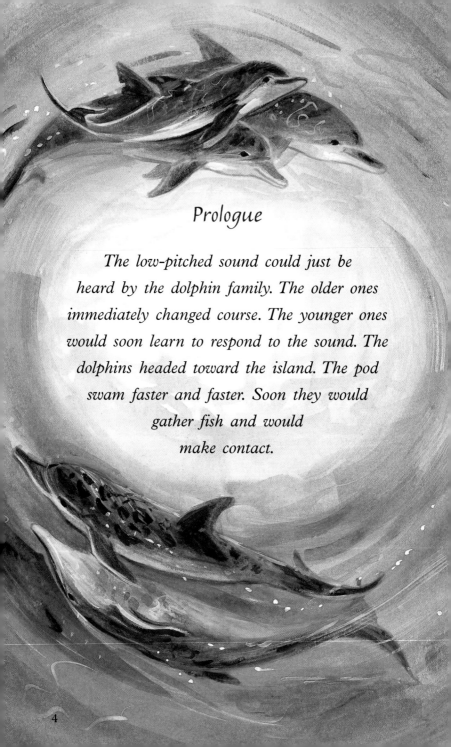

Prologue

The low-pitched sound could just be heard by the dolphin family. The older ones immediately changed course. The younger ones would soon learn to respond to the sound. The dolphins headed toward the island. The pod swam faster and faster. Soon they would gather fish and would make contact.

Chapter One

I guess we all have to die. Particularly old people. But I never thought of Poppy as old. Poppy is my grandfather. But he's more a friend than a grandfather. We've done everything together, ever since I was little. We go fishing a lot. Poppy taught me how to fish. But the best thing about Poppy is his stories. He tells the neatest stories.

Right now, I'm sitting in the waiting room at the hospital. Dad is across from me, staring at the wall. At least I've stopped crying. I just keep thinking that it's my fault. If only we didn't go on that fishing trip...

You see, yesterday, Poppy, my friend Joey, and I motored across to Pelican Island. We were about halfway across when Poppy said, "Do either of you boys want to steer the boat while I get the anchor ready?"

Well, both Joey and I jumped up at the same time. We started to fight over the wheel.

"I was here first!" Joey yelled.

"You can't steer. Anyway it's my Poppy's boat!" I replied.

Joey wouldn't give in. Neither would I. The boat wobbled all over the place.

"Sit down, both of you!" ordered Poppy, as he grabbed the wheel. "I'll fix the anchor as I steer."

We sat quietly for the rest of the trip. I gave Joey an angry look. Joey practically lives at our house. Sometimes he's a real pest. Yet we hang around together all the time. But I don't like sharing Poppy with Joey sometimes.

As we motored in toward the beach, a family of dolphins swam close to the boat. We all started to talk at once.

"Look how close they are!" shouted Joey.

"A sure sign of good luck," Poppy said.

"Hey, that big one has lost a bit of its dorsal fin," I added. There was a notch missing in the middle of its fin. Poppy cut the engine as we glided onto the shore. The dolphins headed back toward deeper water.

"See ya, Notch!" I shouted, thinking I would never see the dolphin again.

We unloaded and set up our tent behind a sand dune. After dinner, Poppy said that he wanted to tell us a story about Pelican Island before we went to bed.

We sat down by the fire. Joey sat really close to Poppy with his mouth open. I think he likes Poppy's stories more than I do!

I thought Poppy's story might be a ghost story. It wasn't, but later, it was this story that would send shivers down my spine. I can't tell stories as well as Poppy, but it went something like this...

Chapter Two

*F*or thousands of years, a tribe of aborigines visited Pelican Island. They stayed a few months each year. They came for the mullet that swam in large schools close to the island.

When the mullet approached the island, the aboriginal elders would go down to the beach and call in the dolphins. The dolphins would herd the school of fish into the shallow water. Then the whole tribe would club and net the fish. They would also feed a few small fish to the dolphins by hand.

Well, a long, long time ago, there were two boys who were members of this tribe. Their names were Manu and Kira. They were cousins of about the same age, and they always played together. Often they explored the island, sharing the food they found, such as turtle eggs or small crabs. They would have pretend battles with spears. Sometimes, when they swam, they would see which one of them could dive the deepest and hold their breath the longest. Manu always came up last.

One day, the boys were collecting shells at the water's edge. As the waves receded, they would dig the shells up from the soft sand with their feet. They were just about to count how many shells they'd found when one of the elders called them from the top of a sand dune. Manu and Kira ran as fast as they could, because the elders were held in the highest respect. They never talked to the children unless it was very important.

Manu and Kira sat down with the elders. They were told that this year they would be asked to call in the dolphins. It would be part of their rite to manhood. If they did this job well, they would be invited to hunt with the men and leave the shell collecting to the women and children.

The boys were extremely proud. It was a great tribal honor to be asked to call in the dolphins. They were shown how to use the "Caller."

The Caller was a large, heavy conch shell, with a small hole in the pointy end. When you blew through the hole, it made a low, haunting sound, like a whale calling its pod.

Just then, a lookout came running, yelling, "Fish! Fish!"

An elder handed the Caller to Manu, and told the boys to go down to the beach and call in the dolphins.

The boys ran into the water up to their waists. The Caller had to be placed with its opening just breaking the surface of the water. As Manu bent over to blow, Kira shouted, "I am older. I should have the first turn!"

"No!" replied Manu. "The Caller was given to me, and I am taller and stronger than you."

Kira ignored him and grabbed the Caller. But Manu ripped it from his grasp and pushed Kira back into the water. Kira became very angry. As Manu bent over again and started to blow into the shell, Kira jumped onto his back. He forced Manu down under the water.

Manu sank, clinging tightly to the shell. Above the surface of the water, Kira heard the bubbles escaping from the shell. He held Manu under until he stopped struggling.

Then he stood back. He couldn't see Manu, even though the water was clear. Kira waited. Suddenly a great wave of shame and loss swept over him as he realized what he had done.

He dived under the water and searched for Manu. Nothing. He surfaced. He knew that not even Manu could hold his breath this long.

Kira punched the surface of the water and started to scream, "Manu! Manu! Oh, Mother of the Ocean, give me back my Manu!"

Suddenly, the water in front of Kira erupted as the body of Manu was pushed through the surface. Kira saw a dolphin lifting him. The dolphin supported Manu under the arm. Manu started to splutter water and began to cough. Kira quickly grabbed him. Slowly, both the dolphin and Kira pushed and pulled Manu to the water's edge.

The two boys were lying on the sand, getting their breaths back, when they heard a "plonk" on the sand between them. The Caller had been thrown back onto the beach! Manu and Kira looked out over the water and saw the dolphin bob its raised head and then disappear.

The elders had watched everything from the top of the dune. They decided that Kira must be punished for trying to drown Manu and nearly losing the Caller. But the elders were unsure how to punish him.

Kira must have control over the ocean for the dolphin to deliver up both Manu and the Caller, the elders thought. The ocean was very powerful, and if Kira were punished too harshly, it might bring great misfortune to the tribe. Finally the elders decided to exile him from the tribe. Kira was sent down to the other end of the island to fend for himself.

Kira was very sad and very lonely for a long time. He was able to find enough food to keep himself alive. But it was very difficult for him when it came time for his tribe to leave the island. He watched from a distance, far down the beach.

As the rest of the tribe boarded the canoes, Manu looked up and saw Kira. He took a few steps toward him, and raised his arm in a goodbye salute. Kira returned the salute. It made him feel much better, knowing his friend had forgiven him.

Kira lived alone on the island for many years. Each year, his tribe returned. And each year, Kira watched them from a distance. He grew close to the dolphins. They were his only friends. He swam with them. He even used to ride them. They provided plenty of fish for him to eat.

Kira did have one more meeting with Manu, but that story will wait for another night.

21

Chapter Three

Joey and I pleaded with Poppy to tell us more, but he said it was late and that we needed to go to bed if we were to get up early and catch the fish. Joey and I hopped into our sleeping bags quickly. But we stayed awake a long time, talking about the island and the fish we were going to catch the next day.

The next morning, while I was sleeping, Joey rose early. He went fishing by himself around the other side of the point. When I finally awoke, Poppy was clearing the breakfast dishes. He asked me to help him carry some gear down to the boat.

We were going to motor around to the point and pick up Joey. I grabbed a piece of toast and a couple of rods, and followed Poppy down to the water.

The boat was anchored just off the beach. Poppy decided to swim out to the boat and then drive it onto the beach to pick up the gear and me. While swimming to the boat, Poppy stopped a couple of times for a rest. I thought it was unusual, because he was usually a strong swimmer.

I began to worry when I saw Poppy struggle to get on board the boat. Then he had trouble starting the outboard motor. He had pulled the starting cord about four times when he suddenly grabbed his chest. He bent over. From the beach, I could see the pain on his face. He then leaned too far to one side of the boat and fell overboard.

"Poppy! Poppy!" I screamed. I couldn't see him. I swam frantically toward the boat. It seemed to take forever to get there. When I finally arrived, there was no sign of him. I checked both sides of the boat. Nothing. I dived under the water. The water was clear. Nothing.

Finally, the thought came to me that Poppy had drowned. I felt very alone. I started to cry while treading water. Then Poppy's story rushed into my head. I suddenly felt angry and, through my tears, I punched the water.

"Poppy! Poppy! Oh, Mother of the Ocean, give me back my Poppy!"

I looked around. I saw a tail flash beneath me. Then a shadow rose from the deep. And, just in front of me, Poppy's head broke the water's surface. A dolphin swam behind him and pushed him toward me. It was Notch, the dolphin I had seen the day before. I was stunned.

I grabbed Poppy. We started to sink, but Notch pushed us back up. I grabbed Poppy's arm and began dragging him toward the beach. Notch kept Poppy above the water by pushing up behind his back. Poppy looked like he was resting on Notch.

Poppy was heavy and it took us a long time to reach the water's edge. Finally I felt sand beneath my feet and I stood up. With Notch still helping, I pulled Poppy clear of the water and laid him on the sand.

Poppy was still unconscious, but I could see his chest moving up and down with small breaths. I rolled him onto his side.

"Wake up, Poppy!" I pleaded. I squeezed his hand. I felt alone again and started to cry.

But then I heard a "plonk" on the sand beside me. I looked out over the water. But I didn't see any dolphins. I turned, and through my tears, saw Joey kneeling beside me.

"What happened?" he asked.

"I think Poppy had a heart attack, and then he nearly drowned," I explained.

"He needs a doctor. There's a boat coming around the point, I'll wave it down!" yelled Joey, and he ran down the beach toward the boat.

Well, Joey did everything else. I was a bit of a mess. I couldn't stop crying. The boat had a radio and it wasn't long before a helicopter landed on the beach and took Poppy to the hospital. And that's where I'm still waiting now.

I haven't told anyone about the dolphin rescue. I don't think they would believe me. I feel so confused. Poppy's story *was* only a story, after all, wasn't it?

Epilogue

A nurse walked into the waiting room. She saw Mr. Ferguson sitting, head bent, and his son, Ricky, sitting opposite him.

"Mr. Ferguson, your father has stabilized. It looks like he'll recover. But no more fishing trips for a while!" she declared.

"Thank goodness!" replied Mr. Ferguson, jumping to his feet.

"He wants to see you, and he especially wants to see his grandson," she said, turning toward Ricky.

The nurse led them to a cubicle at the end of the emergency ward. Ricky ran ahead, but stopped in shock when he saw his grandfather. Wires and tubes covered Poppy's chest.

Ricky walked slowly to Poppy's bed and held his hand. "Hello, Poppy," he whispered.

"Ricky! You saved me," said Poppy, smiling.

"Well, it wasn't just me," Ricky replied.

"You're my hero, Ricky. But how did you get me to shore?" asked Poppy.

Ricky was about to answer, but he saw his father standing on the other side of the bed, and he hesitated.

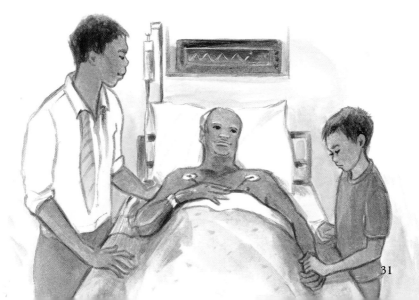

"Oh, Ricky," interrupted Poppy, softly, "I know I must have been dreaming, but when I was falling through the water, I thought I heard someone blowing on a conch shell. Then, suddenly, I felt as if I was riding on a dolphin, up to the surface of the water. It was as if the Mother of the Ocean had tried to save me."

Ricky squeezed his grandfather's hand tightly.